We Eat Dinner in the Bat

by Angela Shelf Medearis

Illustrated by Jacqueline Rogers

Scholastic Reader — Level 2

SCHOLASTIC INC.

New York Toronto London Auckland Sydney
Mexico City New Delhi Hong Kong Buenos Aires

"Do you want to eat dinner at my house, Josh?"

"Okay, Harris."

"We eat dinner in the bathtub."

X-RAY

"THE BATHTUB?"

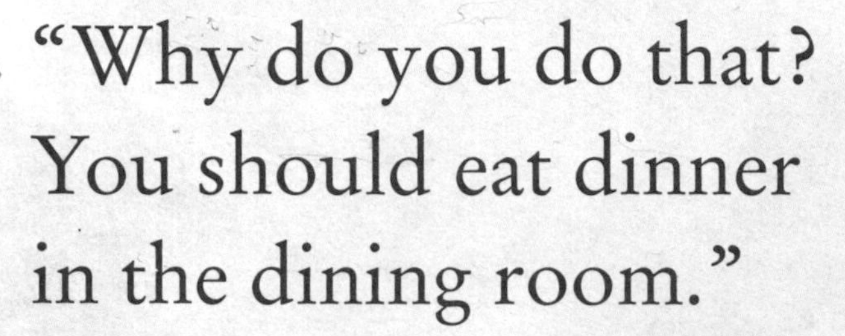

"Yes."

"Why do you do that?
You should eat dinner
in the dining room."

“We sleep in the dining room.”

"Don't you have a bedroom?"

"Yes, we cook in my
bedroom."

"Why don't you cook
in the kitchen?"

"There's no room.
We park our car
in the kitchen."

“Why don’t you park your car in the garage?”

WE LOVE YOU BERT
WE LOVE

"The dog sleeps in there."

"Why don't you put the dog in the backyard?"

“The backyard is filled with—
all kinds of things.”

“Can’t you put all
of those things
in the attic?”

“No, we bathe
in the attic.”

"Why don't you take a bath
in the tub?"
"I told you! 
We eat dinner in the bathtub.
Do you want to eat
with me or not?"

"Okay, but I have to call my mom and let her know. It's my turn to set the table."

"Table? What table?"

“The one in the dining room.”

"Your family eats dinner in the dining room?"

 "Yes."

“That’s what I like
about you, Josh.
You’re so different.”